CHILDHOOD DIAMONDS

ANURAG S PANDEY

ISBN 978-1-68487-376-0

To the child who is still alive in me...

Contents

Acknowledgements

Back Cover Image by Piyapong Saydaung from Pixabay

I
Mindset

Every child takes birth with some diamonds. Those diamonds were to help the child to grow as a complete human being. They could help the child to get rooted deep down and to rise above the sky. They could enlarge the personality of the child in all dimensions. But we don't encourage the child to be careful with those diamonds. Unfortunately we make the child to lose those diamonds. That's why that most of us have lost those diamonds in our childhood. Recollecting them can transform us deeply.

Everyone does have a unique mindset. Mindset plays a major role in the making of life. In the same way the mindset of a country creates that nation and the mentality of a universe drives that universe.

This mind is extremely powerful, not when it plays with us, but when we play with it. Mind can easily control all the elements of nature, if used properly. It is not a miracle at all to create rainfall or to create something out of nothing.

But for an ordinary person mind is just a tool, which makes him or her able to adjust with self, others and everything. In fact mind helps us to survive. A healthy mind is always friendly but when it gets infected, it becomes harmful for self and for others too. It is very rare to find a mind with no complexity. Even a simplest mind on Earth may have multi-personalities. On the other hand a well developed mind may have thousands of independent yet correlated entities. Such a mind can control the mass. A person with such a mind can simultaneously meet thousands of people separately. While in a worst condition a negatively developed mind may have thousands of warriors fighting with each other.

Most people spend their whole lives imprisoned in their individual minds. They never jump beyond their mind and never experience the real world, the real life and the real self.

Up to age of 2-3 years, every kid lives in a very high level of consciousness or you may say that every tiny kid lives with an infinite mind. After that period their mind begins to shrink around worldly thoughts. And in a few years they get captivated in their own mind, which has already become too narrowed, rotating to and fro amid routine thoughts. And this process of narrowing of mind keeps going on. Unfortunately such a mind only is considered a normal mind in our society.

Mind can be developed consciously. By practice one can experience new dimensions of mind. However it may happen unconsciously too. Some outer elements, some event, something may cause it. But unlike consciously developed mind, an unconsciously developed mind can't be controlled by the master of that mind. A man with such a mind is like a drunken driving a brake-less car, or an insane armed with dangerous weapons. Such a mind losses many powers, gains many mysterious powers and behaves weirdly.

Every mind is precious. Every mind has potential to grow positively and beautifully. Even worst kind of mind can be transformed into best one, if given proper nourishment. So recollecting childhood diamonds is an easy way to build a better mind.

In my childhood, I had a sharp but confused mindset. I was genius and fool too. I was Pious, honest, kind, devoted, undisciplined, irregular, flexible and fearful. Some lucky kids do have ability to build their lives by their own, while rest other kids are like soil pots. They depend on potter means outer forces. And I was not a lucky kid. But never happens anything wrong in this world. Everything is on way to its' ultimate goal. Doesn't matter how dark or directionless the way is, it is already leading everyone to their destination. Don't complain that you have all kind of pebbles, stones, sands, dirt and dust. Also some diamonds are there, which you have lost in your childhood. You just need to find them again. You can find them by remembering your childhood. I had many diamonds in my childhood. One of them was **watchfulness**.

II
Watchfulness

I often remember that moment of my childhood. I was 4 years old. My grandmother had taken me to a pond to collect some lotus for worship. I always remember those moments. I was walking towards the pond by holding grandmother's fore-finger. I saw the greeneries and mysterious trees surrounding the pond. I saw the bright white and dark red lotus in the water. I saw the silky waves on the pond surface. I saw my grandmother collecting some flowers. I took one flower in my hand and felt the special touch of it. I sat on the soft wet grass and moved my hand in the water of the pond. I saw the changed pattern of the waves.

You know, I always miss those moments, in which I was a part of a live portrait. I desire to see such scenery again. In later years I saw many ponds, many lotuses. But I could never feel the same, what I had felt that time. The scenery of that small pond seems like it belongs to some different world. So beautiful, so charming, so young, so mysterious and so live... I desire to see such a heavenly pond again. But I know that I have lost the watchful eyes, which I had in my childhood. Without watchful eyes one can never see the real beauty. Without watchful eyes one can never feel the mysterious and heavenly element present in every atom of the existence.

Everything in this existence is just wonderful. You, your feelings, appearing and disappearing of thoughts in your mind, your senses, your family, your house, your locality, street dogs, dust, flowers, wind, your neighbours and strangers... You would find everything just wonderful, if you could get back the watchful eyes, you had in your childhood.

Don't you feel? That you have become unavailable for everything, unavailable for yourself, unavailable for other... That you are living a predicted and predetermined life... We have divided ourselves into many incomplete entities. If we want to recollect ourselves, we have to go back to our childhood, when we were undivided.

Second of those diamonds, I had in my childhood, was **purity**.

III
Purity

I want to share with you a moment of my life when I was eight years old. I had joined a Yoga class and I was excellent in doing some Yoga postures. It was noon. My mom was on a cot keeping clothes in a bag. I was on the same cot watching her. Aside of the cot there was a window. Outside of the window there was a farmhouse whose boundaries were surrounded by different trees. The window had iron bars. For nothing I sat on Padmasana and closed my eyes. With no delay I saw myself going out of the window by floating in the air. I was floating above the trees in the same posture of Padmasana. Iron bars had created no obstacle. The next moment I opened my eyes and found myself seated on the cot only. I was surprised. And I tell you, I was not doing any kind of meditation.

One, who practices meditation, knows that it was an experience of deep meditation, when the practitioner gets able to interact with his or her subtle or astral body. After 10 years I got some interest towards meditation. I practiced meditation for years. And despite all my desire and efforts I could interact with my subtle body a few times only.

What was the reason behind this? In the age of eight I experienced something with no effort and no desire. And later I couldn't experience the same thing despite a lot of efforts!

I think if a man from ten thousand years back is brought to present time and is made to stand on a high traffic road; the man would die in a few minutes. Yes! He will die due to polluted air! But we survive. If a saint is forced to live with body of a common man, with mindset of a common man, with vibration of a common man; the saint would commit suicide. But we live a normal life. In the first example polluted is air and in second example polluted are common man's body, mindset and vibration.

If unpolluted at the level of body, mind and soul, a man would feel light. He would be able to interact with higher self and almighty. He would feel oneness with nature. He would experience the state of deep meditation without trying hard. Unfortunately, in our society a growing child is in process of getting polluted at all levels.

We separate things, humans, families, nations and societies. But in reality nothing is separate, even a drop of water. Everything is attached to each other and affects each other. Their bond continuously creates chain of actions and reactions. If you eat polluted grains, it pollutes your cells. Polluted thoughts are roaming in air. If you receive them; and you receive them if you are unaware, they pollute your thoughts.

I love jungles. I visit jungles whenever I get time. Each time as I enter the jungle, I feel very light and healthy. My palms become reddish. Why? Does it happen so because there is less air pollution? Yes! But there is a bigger cause too behind this. In the jungles there is no crowd of peoples. It means there in the jungles, the vibrations of peoples' thoughts are in very less quantity. So in the jungles I receive less quantity of thoughts' vibrations, which makes me to feel lighter and healthier.

So you are getting polluted by food, water, air and vibrations of peoples' thoughts and by many more things. By developing strong immune system you can reverse the pollution happening at physical level. And to protect your mind, you have to go deeper in your mind. You have to go beyond thoughts. There you can do healing of thoughts. But you have to reconsider your belief system too, because weakest thought can defeat strongest thought, if it is supported by your belief system.

Can you tell the time without looking at watch? Can you accurately see colours of your distant friend's clothing with your closed eyes? And his or her accurate present location? Can you make your friend to see a visual in his or her inner-vision by secretly transmitting the same visual through your mind? If you can't, then you can do it after some practice.

Present science works on the lowest dimension which is physical level. But our ancient saints used to work on higher dimensions too. They were able to reach to anywhere in no time. Not only this! One Saint could reach to multiple places at the same time. In present too there are many saints, who are able to do this. They don't need a mechanical device to fly or to make something to fly. They do this just by using their mind power. May be in future, science would work at higher dimensions and would make available these techniques to common men. Then anyone would be able to reach to multiple places simultaneously just by using a device. But at present these abilities can't be attained without hard practice.

It is not needed that everyone would attain that higher level of consciousness. At least we should go little higher, so that we could experience little of higher dimensions. Then we can develop gradually.

Third of those diamonds I had in my childhood was an **infinite mind**.

IV
Infinite Mind

My father was a preacher. He used to frequently go to long distances. He used to return after a month or two and stay at home for a couple of days. My age was 5 or 6 years. My family members used to ask to me that when would my father come back home? In those days telephones were not common. We didn't know when he will come. So we used to expect his returning any day, any time after one month. Anyway; when family members used to ask to me to tell that when my father would return home, I used to try to find an answer in my mind. After a state of thoughtlessness for a second or two, I used to tell an answer. Once I said, "Papa will come tomorrow." They asked, "what time?" I thought and replied, "7 o' clock in the evening."

And next day father returned home at sharp 7 PM. And each time they received correct answer from me for next 2-3 years. After that I was not able to deliver them correct answer. Now answer was not coming from the state of thoughtlessness. Now I was creating them in a thoughtful mind. A thoughtful mind is a very limited mind. It can't go beyond your stored knowledge and learned skills, while a thoughtless mind is an infinite mind. It can know each and everything of whole Universe. It can know all secrets and mysteries. It can be attached with anyone's mind. It can reach anywhere. It can travel to past and future. It can go beyond time.

In the later years too some holes had been left unfilled in my limited thoughtful mind, as I was still getting some glimpses of infinite mind. Like once I was talking with one phone friend. I had never seen her. So I tried to see her in my mind. I saw that she was talking to me on cell phone laid on left side of a cot. She was in a red dress. I saw the room very clearly. I asked her and found everything correct. Later she sent me her picture, and I came to know that I had seen the same girl in my mind. She was laid on left side of the cot wearing a red dress.

Once I was talking with my fiancé on cell phone. She was thousands of miles away from me and I was missing her a lot. After disconnecting the call I closed my eyes thinking about her. Suddenly I felt some circulating vibes appeared in my brain for a second. I could also see those vibes. And then only a visual appeared in my brain. She was giving oil massage to her mother's head in the yard. The visual was very clear. That visual disappeared in two-three seconds. I immediately called her back and she got surprised when I told her this. She was still massaging her mother's head.

Once in our workplace I was spending some free time with my friend. I asked him to close his eyes and try to receive the visuals, which I was going to transmit secretly through my mind. I closed my eyes and began to imagine that my consciousness got spread throughout his consciousness. Then I visualized a mountain covered with ice and a lake nearby with a lot of flowers. After some moments I detached myself from him and opened my eyes and asked him too to open his eyes. Then I asked him that did he see something? He described the same visuals.

Once I wanted to heal one friend of mine, who had some skin problem. I wanted to do distant healing without telling her. Visibly I was not very close to her. But inside I was deeply attached with her. Suddenly I saw some mysterious visuals like some spirits were protecting the girl or what I don't know. Then I felt a very different and unfamiliar fragrance around me. I felt the fragrance for a few minutes long. Next day in my workplace as I went near her, the same fragrance moved around me. I was puzzled. I had come near her many times before and I had never received that fragrance before this. I have had more than hundreds of such experiences. But it is not needed to tell each one of them in this book. So I move ahead.

Feeling of innocence and guilt are two strong emotions, which deeply affect us. Feeling of guilt creates storm in the ocean of mind, while feeling of innocence calms down that ocean. Both feelings are very important because feeling of guilt throws out your impurities and feeling of innocence brings you closer to yourself. But this will happen only if these both feelings are justified. Unknowingly we often create unjustified feelings of innocence and guilt. Unjustified feeling of innocence takes us farther from our self, while unjustified feeling of guilt makes us more impure.

One may have feeling of innocence while killing an animal for religious activities. That will be an unjustified feeling of innocence. One may have feeling of guilt if fails to donate gold's cat after unknowingly killing a cat. Also this will be an unjustified feeling of guilt. If you could get back your childhood heart, you would find that most of your feelings of innocence and guilt are unjustified. This is the reason that we are getting more impure and getting farther from ourselves.

A child does have a free soul. A child is free from social, moral and religious boundaries. A child is free from helplessness of worldly cunningness. A child doesn't need to earn money or buy homes. A child doesn't need to exploit others or to try to save self from getting exploited. So a child's feeling of innocence and guilt are always justified, unless we force the child to start becoming like us. And by that point a child starts getting impure and farther from self. Actually we corrupt a child's feeling.

Fourth of those diamonds I had in childhood was an **innocent mind**.

V

Innocent Mind

My age was 4 or 5 years. In those days fourth day moon shaped biscuit were sold in shops. I liked that biscuit very much. Mother used to keeps coins in a basket. She used to give coins to my elder sister. Sister used to take me to a shop, which was just in beside of our house. She used to buy one biscuit for me by giving one coin to the shopkeeper. Once I wanted to taste that fourth day moon shaped biscuit. Mother was busy in kitchen and sister was not at home. I went beneath the cot and took out the basket and took one coin from that. I went to the shop and handed the coin to the shopkeeper and asked one biscuit of my choice. Shopkeeper gave me two biscuits. But I returned one and returned home eating one biscuit. After some time that shopkeeper came to my house and told my mother that I bought one rupee biscuit from him and gave him two rupee coin. He returned one rupee to my mother. I was watching this all while eating the biscuit. Mother told the shopkeeper that she didn't give me money. She checked the basket and found one coin missing. Mother, shopkeeper and neighbours came to a conclusion that I stole the coin for biscuit. But that was not the truth. I didn't steal the coin. I took the coin because I knew that coin has ability to get me biscuit. I had no feeling of guilt at all. Even today when I remember that event, I feel no guilt. But in later years whenever I secretly took some money from house for fulfilling some of my needs, each time I felt guilty, because I had been told that stealing money is a sin, is an immoral act.

Knowledge of good and bad makes the difference to what we feel. Unfortunately most of that knowledge misleads us and is needed to be reconsidered. We live in nature. We should go with natural feelings, not educated feelings. We should give importance to natural things like bread and hunger, love and joy and so on. And we should not give unnecessary importance to unnatural things like money, status etc. If you are natural, then your feelings of innocence and guilt will always be justified. In fact if you are natural, you would get rid of feeling of guilt, because then you won't do anything wrong deliberately. So a child rarely feels guilty. But we corrupt child's feeling of innocence and guilt by giving him the knowledge of good and bad.

Also consciousness plays major role in creation of feelings in our mind. Same repeated act with different level of consciousness will create different type of feelings. If a boy hugs a girl with lower level of consciousness, the boy will feel lust. If the same boy hugs the same girl with little higher level of consciousness, he will feel no lust but a friendly attachment with that girl. And if the same boy hugs the same girl with little extra higher level of consciousness, he will feel unconditional love for that girl. If the boy increases his level of consciousness further, he will feel oneness with the girl. With further higher consciousness level, he will feel divinity. He will feel as if he is hugging the nature, as if he is hugging the God.

But that boy can raise the level of his consciousness, only if he tries to reconsider the knowledge of good and bad, what he is given by the society. He has been taught to feel lust for a girl. He has to drop that knowledge. Then he can explore the true knowledge of good and bad. Then his feeling of innocence and guilt will be justified.

Do you really live in this World or you have kept yourself separate from everyone and everything and meet the World only your thought process? While interacting with something or someone, thought process creates an image of that thing or person. And that image can never tell you exactly about that thing or person. And often that image gives you wrong or surface information. Thought process makes you to remain unknown to everything and everyone, even to yourself too. You don't know the exactly you because not you but your thought process meets you.

A tiny child knows the World better than elders. A tiny child is untouched by thought process. A child meets everything with an open heart. Then we force the child to learn thought process. And gradually the child closes his heart and becomes unknown to self. The real self of the child gets locked in the deepest of his heart and the child becomes just a thought process like us.

Fifth of those diamonds I had in childhood was an **open heart**.

VI
Open Heart

Nature understands the language of heart. It never listens to the language of brain. Only with an open heart you can communicate with nature. All mysteries of nature are openly spread throughout. But they are mysteries because you cannot see them without an open heart. In each one of us, there is great attraction and desire for God or something like God. Do you know why? Because there is Godly thing or God matter in deepest of us. With an open heart we naturally begin to emit that God energy or Godly love all around even unknowingly. With an open heart we accept everyone and everything without any logical calculation. Since, you are emitting God energy or Godly love, so everyone around you feels great attraction towards you. Since, you accept everyone, so you become accepted by everyone. That is the reason that a small child receives love and acceptance from everyone except those who have zero or negative humanity.

I remember when I was a small child, everyone used to love me, kiss me and I remained thoughtless for them. Some of them were rich and some were poor. Some were beautiful and some were less beautiful. Some were good hearted and some were less good-hearted. But I reflected no difference. I accepted each one of them equally. Perhaps the God inside me had seen the same God inside them.

We take child's activities as childish activities. But if you would see carefully, you would find that elders' activities are more childish. Imagine that the person in front of you is a child. Then observe that person's activities carefully. His egoistic talk, his efforts to prove himself a Wiseman, his quarrels, his effort to present bad as good and good as bad, his flirting, his cheating… You would surprisingly know that the person in front of you is so childish. Then you would not feel bad on his bad talks, rather you would laugh. And if you would take the person in front of you as a child, that person would feel himself as a child. He would meet you with an open heart.

Perhaps a child takes everyone in front of him as a child, and so elders feel like a child when they go close to a child. Child's natural energy inspires elders' energy. It is said that God lives in child. God may live in you too, if you could get back those diamonds which you had in your childhood.

I had many more diamonds in my childhood. But in this book I shall tell you about one more. Sixth of those diamonds I had in my childhood was **originality**.

VII
Originality

It is tough to find original stuff, whether you buy milk, wine, medicine or eatables. Nothing is original. But what about yourself? Are you original? Do you display the real you? Or do you even know the real you? Your real character? Definitely no! Whom, you would honestly take the real you, would be a mix-up of several inspired, influenced, created, artificial, desired and imagined characters. A child lives in his real character. A child takes birth naked and he has nothing to hide. And he doesn't show anything artificial. When he laughs, he really laughs. When he cries, he really cries. When he sleeps, he really sleeps. When he plays, he really plays. What about you?

A child lives in his absolute originality, untouched by religion and caste, untouched by wealth and poverty, untouched by status, customs and boundaries. Then gradually we teach him everything. Some of those teachings are necessary, some are unnecessary and some are dangerous, which pollute child's character and personality. It is good to inspire the child to respect elders, but by heart. And it is bad to force the child to touch each and every elder's feet. In this case the child will learn to touch elders' feet with disrespect in his heart. It is good to inspire the child to do his best while preparing for the School exams. But it is bad to force the child to attain highest marks in the class. In this case, if child succeeds, he will become egoistic. And if he fails, he will develop inferiority complexity. It is good to teach the child knowledge of your religion. But it is bad to teach him hatred for other religions.

And never think that you teach the child only in direct way! Child learns from your expressions, activities and talks. If someone is saying to someone that someone is bad and a child happens to hear this, the child creates a negative image of that person about whom both were talking. If a child hears elders' hateful talks against some group or religion, that enters child's belief system. When that child grows young, he feels hatred for that group or religion. He never comes to know that there is no reason behind his hatred, except one, that in his childhood he had heard elders' hateful talks against that group or religion.

Child observes elders saying one thing and doing another thing. Child observes his father behaving as cobra in front of wife, behaving as fox in front of society, behaving as lion in front of helpless and behaving as pet dog in front of authorities. The child observes all kind of activities of elders. He learns the same things unknowingly. And gradually his originality of character gets contaminated. If you want to regain your originality of character, then you have to seek with burning desire, you have to seek for that untouched you, unpolluted you, unconditioned you, who is free from all boundaries.

℘

VIII
Childhood Explained

Your childhood can help you to become the real you. It can influence you to unfold your potentials. It can guide you to attain your real qualities. But you too have to understand your childhood, good and bad sides of your childhood. My childhood explained will help you to understand your childhood in a new way. It will also help you to give better nourishment to the children around you.

I was an all time thin but strong guy. I think that my higher self had stopped at the age of 7. It means even after getting an adult, I was a 7 years old boy internally. Not physically, not mentally, but in the deepest of my heart and soul I remained a child. I used to refuse this fact and tried to become an adult internally too. But all went in vain. I remained a child at my higher consciousness level. And that child used to show his presence through my expressions, thinking and talking. Despite all of my efforts, everyone who interacted with me came to know that I was a child. Those, who were gentle, behaved nicely with me. Those, who were soft-hearted, loved me. Those, who were spiritual, respected me. Those, who were innocent, befriended with me. Those peoples, who had negative energy, they be fooled me, cheated me, exploited me, threatened me. But I had good feeling and best wishes for everyone. Being a child at my higher consciousness level, I was unable to think bad for anyone. I am thankful to God that my heart remained a child's heart. Due to that I couldn't gain many worldly successes. But a child's heart is more precious than worldly successes. Though I always felt lack of commonsense in me.

Lack of commonsense is generally understood a light, funny and bad quality. In fact it affects the life very badly. With lack of commonsense, you can't use your knowledge and skills properly. With lack of commonsense you can't express yourself in right manner. With lack of commonsense your thought process cannot be at ease and you use to undergo unnecessary emotions like fear, anxiety, doubt, irritation, anger, distrust etc. With lack of commonsense you can't maintain relationships in a healthy way. You can't see things as they are. You cannot plan and manage your life in any way.

I was 4 years old. A kid of same age asked me, "Do you know the spelling of car?" That kid had average IQ, while I had more than average IQ. I thought "Car" means "Ambassador". And I didn't know the spelling of Ambassador. So I replied, "No! I don't know the spelling of car." That kid said, "It's so simple. C A R car". I realized my mistake but I couldn't develop commonsense even in the next two decades.

I was five years old. My mother was a teacher in the same school in which I was a student. In the classroom I felt urgent need for motion. It was more than one hour for the final bell. I couldn't make my mind to tell the teacher that I need to go for toilet. Somehow I controlled till the final bell. Then we moved for home. One lady teacher was with my mother. The way from school to home was about one kilometre. We were going on feet. Due to the presence of that lady teacher I couldn't make my mind to tell my mother about my urgent need for the release of motion. I controlled my best but failed. When mother noticed my condition, she took necessary steps.

In the age of three I was in nursery classroom. My middle-aged fat lady teacher called me and asked me to read alphabets. Perhaps I was not in mood to read alphabets or perhaps I couldn't get her or perhaps I needed some time. But with no patience she tweaked my ear. While she was tweaking my ear, I was realizing that she was punishing me for no mistake. And that moment only I created a mindset against school. I started to try my best to escape school. And this continued for next seven years. I applied hundreds of funny, weird, brilliant, dangerous and unique ideas for escaping school.

Once I decided to finish myself so that I could get rid of school forever. I put stones on the ground and set on edge of the roof. Stones were for assured death. None had any idea about what was running in my mind. However I couldn't make my heart to jump down. Then I hit on my chest with stone many times, so that some severe health issue would give me rid of school for many days. But nothing happened except some swelling. I told nothing to none.

Once while I was unwillingly stepping towards the school, I stopped in half-way in front of a house. Men and women were seated on cots. A woman asked to me, "what happened?" With a painful face, tearful eyes and chocking voice I asked, "May I sit here?" They worriedly helped me to sit on a cot. I told them that my heart is paining. They got panicked and sent someone to inform my family. My family members came hurriedly. They took care of me and took me back to home. I had got rid of school for one day.

When I completed my six years, I was given responsibility to bring sweet water from a neighbour's house, which was at 200 meters distance. Sweet water was necessary for cooking pulses. Family members used to force me to bring sweet water when I used to watch my favourite cartoon show. I had no mindset to refuse or to talk logically. Each time I unwillingly went to bring the sweet water. Family members had no idea about my intense unwillingness and irritation. The whole way to that neighbour's house, I used to abuse my family members in murmuring way. And when I took water from the hand pump, I used to release all my irritation by spitting into the water of pot, "You dirty peoples! Send me to bring water! Don't let me watch my favourite cartoon show. Am I your servant? Can't you bring water yourself! You will eat my spitted pulses. Spit... Spit... Spit..." This spitting went on for next 2-3 years. When after 5-6 years I told my family about this spitting story, they laughed aloud and said, "Why didn't you refuse? Or you could go after the cartoon show." If one could learn to express his or her unwillingness in clear words, he or she would not have to carry tons of irritation. If he or she doesn't learn this for long time, then he or she would create a habit of unwillingness and irritation. His or her relationship with others will become complex, impractical and abnormal. The same had happened with me.

In early age of 12 I developed interest towards novels. I read many good and bad novels. Some of them touched me deeply while some destroyed my time and energy. Every reading affects on readers' personality. Unfortunately I read great and cheap both types of novels. Great novels inspired me and cheap one influenced me to think impractically, to see far from the reality, to act baselessly. At first I decided to become an army-man. When I came to know that my height is less than army's requirement, I decided to become a detective. Without trying hard for that after some time I decided to become a lyricist. After some vain efforts, I decided to become a businessman, then social worker, then computer scientist, then hypnotist, then philosopher... I desired and imagined about each of those characters. But I did little or no ground level preparation. As a result when the real time came to do something and when I was thrown alone in front of the real world, I found myself unfit for each of those characters, what I wanted to become. To survive I had to do petty jobs as salesman, private tutor etc. I had lost the battle of life and life's dreams. I failed to use my qualities. I failed to develop my skills. I had excellent knowledge in many fields but no mastery in any. I had to make a new start.

This is not only my story. This could be your story too. There may be some exceptions. Otherwise this is our story. We want to become someone. We try to become someone else. And we become someone else. We may or may not realize. But it is truth that we are not using our skills properly. We are not doing for what we have taken this birth. Childhood Diamonds will certainly help you to rebuild, reform and reshape yourself.

ABOUT THE AUTHOR

Anurag S Pandey

Anurag S Pandey is a writer, poet and computer programmer. His poems have been published in national newspapers and magazines of India like Navbharat Times, Kadambini etc. He has written Story/ Screenplay/ Dialogues for various TV Shows like Lady Inspector, Shaka Laka Boom Boom, Indonesian TV shows etc. At present he lives in Bhubaneswar, India. Meditation, yoga, mystery, paranormal & supernatural activities are some of his favorite topics to read and write.

Other Books by the Author:

- Adhoori Kavitaayen / अधूरी कविताएँ

- Fitoor… / फ़ितूर…: Anurag S Pandey ki Aprasiddha Kahaaniyaan
- Fitoor: A Collection of Nine Unique, Adorable and Inspirational Short Stories
- Good, Evil and Supernatural (Hindi Edition)
- Good, Evil & Supernatural…: Tales of unsolved mysteries
- Let's Play with Excel: 51 original & useful macros
- Develop Snake & Ladder Game in an Hour: Complete Guide with Code & Design
- The bull named Milton was born to win the race.: a comedy thriller screenplay

Available on Amazon, Apple books, Smashwords, Kobo, Scribd, Barnesandnoble, Google Play and Notion Press. Author used his name as Anurag Pandey also.

Some Links of the Author's Books:
https://notionpress.com/author/397403
https://www.amazon.in/~/e/B083STJ8F8
https://www.smashwords.com/profile/view/ANURAGPANDEY
https://www.kobo.com/in/en/search?query=anurag%20pandey&fcsearchfield=Author
https://books.apple.com/au/author/anurag-pandey/id818684991
https://www.scribd.com/author/518186969/Anurag-Pandey
https://www.barnesandnoble.com/w/just-for-fun-anurag-pandey/1137674263
https://play.google.com/store/books/author?id=ANURAG+S+PANDEY

ॐ

ABOUT THE AUTHOR

Mailing Address:
Anurag S Pandey
Near Vishnu Mandir, BDA Colony, Sri Hari Vihar,
Jatni, Khurda, India - 752050
Email Addresses:
anurag_k_p@yahoo.co.in
anuragspandey@gmail.com
Face book Profile: https://www.facebook.com/
anurag.pandey.98031
Face book Page:https://www.facebook.com/
HalfCoockedThoughts/?ref=bookmarks
Twitter:https://twitter.com/ANURAGP64628371

Printed by Libri Plureos GmbH in Hamburg,
Germany